FLIGHT OF T

A Fenland Adventure

by Rosemary Hayes

Anglia Young Books

About the Author

Rosemary Hayes lives and works in East Anglia. She has written several information books for children and her first children's novel, RACE AGAINST TIME, was runner-up for the Kathleen Fidler Award in 1987.

First published in 1989
by Anglia Young Books
Durhams Farmhouse, Ickleton
Saffron Walden, Essex CB10 1SR

Illustrations by Edward Blake

Design and production in association with
Book Production Consultants
47 Norfolk Street
Cambridge CB1 2LE

British Library Cataloguing in Publication Data
Hayes, Rosemary
  Flight of the mallard.
  I. Title
  823'.914 [J]

ISBN 1-871173-06-X

Typeset in 10½/12½ point Palatino by Witwell Ltd, Southport
and printed in Great Britain by
Redwood Press Limited, Melksham, Wiltshire.

AUTHOR'S NOTE

In 1630, The Earl of Bedford and some other "adventurers" undertook to drain the fens. They agreed to pay for the drainage in return for a large part of the reclaimed land.

Sir Cornelius Vermuyden, a Dutch engineer, was invited to supervise the work and, at the time of this story (1631), the Old Bedford River was being dug, from Earith to Salters Lode, near Denver. It is called the Old Bedford because it soon became clear that one drain was not enough, so another larger drain was cut, parallel with the first. This was called the New Bedford.

Both the New and Old Bedford Rivers can still be seen today.

From the start, drainage work was hampered by the shortage of money and equipment. It was also often sabotaged by the fendwellers. But in 1637, despite all these problems, Vermuyden declared that the job was finished and the fens were drained. But he was over-optimistic and it was soon obvious that his dykes and drains and sluices were not coping with the huge drainage job.

Of course, Vermuyden was bitterly disappointed – and so was King Charles, who had planned to build a town in the fens. The King himself then made sure that the work continued, but he soon had other problems and in 1642 England was plunged into Civil War.

After the end of the war, the work went on and on 25th March 1653, Vermuyden once again declared the drainage complete.

This time he was right, but this massive scheme caused another, quite different problem. The drained peat soil started to shrink and dry out and, as it shrank, it became lower, making it very difficult to get the water up into the rivers and out to sea. At first, windmills kept the water levels under control. Later, these were replaced by steam pumps and, later still, by electricity.

The battle to keep the fens dry goes on, even today. But because of Vermuyden's work and the work of those who came after him, the fens now have some of the richest farming land in Britain.

• • • • •

The story of Peter and his family is pure fiction, but the fen people did violently oppose the draining of the fens and resented the presence of Vermuyden and his "foreign" workers.

No-one knows exactly where Vermuyden lived while he supervised the draining, but it is thought that he may have had a house at Fen Drayton. We know that his eldest son, Cornelius, was baptised in London in March 1626, so at the time of the story (1631) he would have been about six years old.

I should like to thank Mike Petty of the Cambridgeshire Collection and Margaret Smith of the Schools Library Service (Fenland area) for providing material for this book, Jenny Anderson for her splendid research work and Nicholas James for checking the manuscript.

CHAPTER ONE

Peter scowled as he guided the sharp-nosed punt expertly along secret channels known only to fendwellers like himself. He kept close to the reeds, a stealthy silent hunter, knowing every bird call, every sound on the wind and recognising even the faintest rustle on the humpy waterlogged islands he passed.

It was springtime; the dreadful fen winter was over and the biting winds, swirling fogs and rising damp had gone. Yet, despite the bright sky and the new growth, Peter could not shake off his dark mood. He felt a constant gnawing anger – an anger which was shared by all the fendwellers.

At first there had been a rumour, brought back from the big market at the edge of the fens where the fendwellers went to sell what they could – goose feathers, eggs, reeds for thatching, or a kreel of fish. Peter remembered the day his sister, Meg, had come back, wide-eyed with news.

'Father!' she said, stumbling into the gloomy little house. 'Father! There's talk all over the market. They're going to drain the fens! What does it mean?'

Their father had just returned from hunting and he put a brace of wildfowl down in front of him and then carefully placed two eggs beside them. He smiled at Meg's flushed face:

'There's been talk of drainage these many years past,' he said. 'They'll never do it. Only fen people understand this land.'

But the rumours wouldn't die and, as time went on, the fen people went more often to the market to learn what they could, ignoring the insults hurled at them from the uplanders – the folk who lived on dry land:

'Yellowbellies!'
'Slodgers!'
'Webfeet!'

One day, Peter's father went himself. He was gone all day and when at last they heard the swish of his punt his family went out and stood waiting for him. Peter's mother held onto his sister for support, for she was again gripped by the fen ague, her body shaken with fever.

There was silence as they watched him tie up the punt and walk wearily towards them; silence broken only by lapping water and an occasional bird call.

'It's true,' he said at last. 'This time it's true.' And his voice was full of hatred and bewilderment.

Peter's mother whispered:

'What will it mean for us?'

Peter's father laughed – a laugh that was harsh and without humour:

'I'll tell you what it will mean,' he said. 'It will mean the end of our life here.'

'But how can that be?'

Peter's father sighed:

'If they succeed in draining this land and turning it into farmland, we shall have no food. No fish, no wildfowl, no eels – nothing. No reeds, no peat – nothing.'

Peter's mother was seized by another fit of shaking, and when she could speak, her words came out in gasps:

'But if it becomes good farmland, perhaps we could grow crops and raise cattle,' she suggested.

Peter was watching his father and he saw the pulse in his temple beating and his face flush a deep red. He knew those signs and instinctively he backed away. But his father's anger wasn't directed at any of them.

'Crops!' he shouted. 'Crops!' 'Oh yes, crops will be grown here alright. But not by us. Not by the people who have always lived here – whose land it is by right. Not by the fen people.'

'Who by, then?' asked Peter.

His father turned to him. His face relaxed and he put an arm round his son's shoulder. In a quieter voice he said:

'If these fens are drained, then the farmland will be given to the people who have paid for the draining.'

'What!'

Peter's father nodded:

'The Earl of Bedford and his rich friends; the fourteen Adventurers.' He spat out the words. 'They will raise the money to pay for the drainage and they will reap the rewards.'

'But who will work for them?' said Peter's mother. 'Surely no fendwellers will dig for them?'

'Oh no!' said Peter's father. 'No fendweller wants to see his livelihood destroyed. In any case, a traitor would soon find his throat slit.' 'No,' he went on, 'The Earl and his Adventurers have brought outsiders here to do the job. People who care nothing for the fens!'

Later that night, Peter had gone with his father to set eel traps. His father had been moody and silent and Peter knew better than to break that silence, so they worked together for a long time without speaking.

Then, at last, his father said:

'How old are you, boy?'

'Twelve,' replied Peter, without hesitating.

Although he could neither read nor write, he could count, and he knew he had been born in the spring. Each spring his mother had notched a mark on a special willow tree and now there were twelve marks.

'Twelve, eh?' said his father. 'And already doing man's work.'

Peter was pleased and smiled into the darkness. But his father's next remark took him by surprise:

'You may have to do more man's work, soon.' He stopped, searching for the right words. Then he said, carefully: 'I may be not be able to fish and hunt for the family. Soon I shall have to do other work and you will have to take on my jobs.'

Peter was puzzled: 'What other work, father?'

But his father didn't answer the question and instead told him to start checking the traps.

As they glided back to the house in the early dawn, Peter, shivering with cold, looked at the writhing, slithering eels in the bottom of the punt.

'There'll be no more eels, if they drain the fens,' he said, almost to himself. Then, to his father:

'Can they really do it, father?'

Peter's father stopped punting for a moment and looked across the huge expanse of water, gleaming in the cold dawn light and broken up by reeds and islands. When the summer came, some of it would be dry again, dry enough to graze cattle and sheep, but it was impossible ever to imagine it as real farmland. He leant on his punt pole and sighed:

4

'They're going to try and drain it, no doubt about that. But they won't succeed.'

'What can stop them?'

Peter's father pulled up the punt pole and then gave a savage push so that they sped silently onwards:

'What can stop them?' He laughed – that harsh humourless laugh:

'The weather can stop them, Peter. These foreigners know nothing of the winter aegar.'

Peter nodded. He had seen what the aegar could do; the aegar was when the wind and the water combined forces to break river banks and destroy homes. Their last home had been a victim of the winter aegar.

Then, almost to himself, Peter's father muttered:

'There'll be more than weather to hinder their work. The fenmen will see to that.'

• • • • •

All that was months ago. Now it was spring again and Peter was thirteen.

A lot had happened in a year. The draining had begun and gangs of diggers and bankers were a familiar sight as they worked on the great Bedford dyke, which was to be over twenty miles long, going in a straight line from Earith to Salter's Lode, near Denver, with many sluice gates and drains in between. And at Salter's Lode, the biggest sluice of all would be built, its job to carry water from the fen rivers directly out to sea and to hold back the tides that surged from the sea down into the river Ouse and thence to flood the fenlands.

During the harsh fen winter, when no digging could be

5

done, the workers had been under cover, making sluice gates and weaving huge mats of osiers which would be covered with clay to strengthen the steep banks of the dyke.

And during that year, the name of one man had become the name most hated by all the fendwellers.

Vermuyden. Sir Cornelius Vermuyden, the Dutch engineer who was overseeing the whole operation. He was clever and he was single-minded. He had successfully drained another tract of land in England and King Charles had knighted him for his work. Vermuyden was determined to succeed in draining the fens.

• • • • •

Peter had had a good day's hunting. Fish and snared wildfowl lay in the bottom of the punt and it was still early. He pushed his punt pole into the mud and sat silent, hidden from view by a clump of reeds.

'Vermuyden,' he whispered to the water beneath him. What chance did the fendwellers stand against him? The Dutchman had guessed that there would be trouble. He had guards posted all along the banks of the dyke for he knew exactly what the fenmen were up to. It was true that a few of the guards had been taken unaware – silently garotted while the fenmen went swiftly about their dangerous business, blowing holes in the dyke. But the fenmen had often been caught.

Peter shivered, despite the warmth of the sun. He feared for his father, out of the house so often now on mysterious business. Although he said nothing, Peter knew he was a fen tiger, a fenman determined to stop the draining. How long would it be before his own father was caught and flung into jail?

He set off slowly towards home, then, on a sudden impulse, he changed direction. It was still early. No need to go just yet. It was a long time since he'd visited the digging – not since the previous summer. He wanted to see for himself what progress had been made and what the fen tigers were really up against.

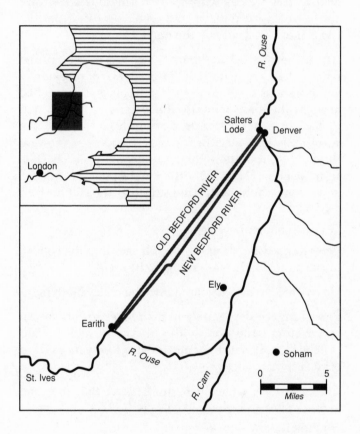

CHAPTER TWO

Cautiously, Peter slid past reeds and willows, always keeping quiet and out of sight. He lived and breathed the fens – for he had known no other home – but the wild watery wastes with their treacherous bogs were also a haven for outlaws and criminals, safe from the law if they could survive the harsh life.

At last he reached the mere which led to the ground where they were digging. He hid his punt skilfully among some reeds and took out his stilts. He had brought them today in case the water was low enough to try out some of the tracks which lay beneath the surface of the water; firm grassy tracks criss-crossing the fens. If you knew them, you could walk on stilts from island to island. Still sitting in the punt, he prodded down beneath the water and smiled as the stilt hit firm ground.

'It's safe enough now Peter.'

Peter jumped and dropped the stilt back into the bottom of the punt. There was no-one to be seen!

He twisted round and stared into the reeds. Nothing!

Peter fumbled desperately in his pocket for his special charm stone – the stone with a hole in the middle – and clutched it as he fearfully muttered the prayers to ward off evil spirits.

Then the voice came again, much closer this time, and another punt shot alongside his own.

'You foolish boy. It's only me!'

Peter let out a sigh of relief, dropped the charm stone back into his pocket and smiled. It was his father's friend, Old George, respected by all who knew him for his skill at handling a punt and stalking his prey. He was known as "Old George" because he was twisted and misshapen from rheumatism, but he was no older than Peter's father.

'What are you doing here, boy,' he said, in his hoarse voice. 'Are you spying on those foreigners?'

Peter grinned. Old George hated them as much as Peter's father.

'I want to see how far they've got.'

'Then we'll go together,' said George. 'I've got my stilts.'

When the punts were both well hidden, they set off. Peter took with him a couple of mallard eggs, still warm from the nest. Away from home, it was always wise to have a gift to exchange. The uplanders had many things that fendwellers found useful but couldn't make for themselves, and sometimes eggs or birds or fish could be exchanged for a tool or a piece of cloth.

They didn't talk as they made their way, in single file, across the mere. Soon they could see the gangs of workmen in the distance.

'So many of them,' thought Peter.

Reaching firm land, they hid their stilts, but their broad muddy feet still betrayed them as fenmen. They walked up the side of an open drain towards the main dyke.

Peter shaded his eyes and stared. The new dyke stretched far into the distance, straight as an arrow – and so wide! Seventy foot wide, it was rumoured, and Peter could believe it.

'Its gone so far!' said Peter and, beside him, he could feel

George's anger.

'They say the Dutchman is displeased; he thinks progress is too slow, though it's a lot too fast for us. But what can we do? We risk our lives to destroy a bit here, a bit there, but they rebuild it. They are making good progress.'

'Who are those people?' asked Peter suddenly. In the distance, a group of horsemen had appeared, riding along the side of the dyke. Peter and George watched them as they came closer, then reined in to talk to one of the foremen. There were two men and with them a boy of about Peter's age and another, much younger boy, mounted on a stocky pony.

There was a sharp intake of breath, then George whispered:

'Sweet heaven, it's him! Vermuyden himself!'

'Vermuyden! How do you know? Which one?'

George pointed to one of the riders:

'I've seen him once before,' he muttered. 'It's not a face I'd forget.'

Peter stared at the figure on horseback, at his tall black hat, his pointed beard, the white lace at his neck and wrists, and his fur jacket.

So this was the man that was turning their lives upside down. Had he any idea what he was doing to the fen-dwellers? Peter spat in the direction of the Dutchman and George smiled approvingly.

'Who are the others?' asked Peter. 'Are those boys his sons?'

George shrugged: 'I don't know. I heard he's brought his family to these parts now; he's built a Dutchified house at Fen Drayton.'

Peter looked curiously at the two boys in their quality clothes and then back at his own chapped hands and mud-caked legs.

'They sit there like stupid fancy ducks!' he said scornfully.

'Like mallard. Puffed-up mallard,' said George, cackling with laughter; then abruptly the laughter stopped and George was wracked by a fit of coughing. His eyes bulged and his thin chest heaved with effort. Peter stood by helplessly. When at last the coughing stopped, he said:

'Have you tried the wise woman's cures?'

George nodded:

'Last winter when I was trembling with the ague, I took the spider cure,' he said. 'That sent the ague away. And I have moles' feet round my neck and a garter of eelskin for my rheumatism, but nothing seems to cure this cough.'

Peter knew about the spider cure. His mother had tried it. For days she had a live spider in a bag round her neck but the ague still tortured her. Poppy tea was the only thing that helped his mother, but then it left her addle-headed.

George seemed to read his thoughts:

'They say the wise woman has a new cure for the ague now.'

'What is it?' said Peter. 'Can we get it for my mother?'

George looked doubtful, then he smiled:

'There's nothing to be lost by going to see the wise woman,' he said, 'though we haven't much to give her. I suspect she'll want a lot in exchange.'

'I've got some eggs,' said Peter.

'And I have some wildfowl,' said Geroge, patting the bag tied round his waist.

They walked together towards the village, slowly, for George could not go for long without gasping. Everywhere, they saw the foreigners, chatting to the upland farmers in the market, buying provisions or going in and out of the inn. The village had prospered because of them – and especially the innkeeper.

'He doesn't care about the fens,' said George. 'All he cares about is making money. Why, he's never got his feet wet in his life!'

'The foreigners can't *all* live at the inn!' said Peter.

George smiled: 'No. Some are building their own houses. Some live on boats. They come and go. A lot of them couldn't stand the winter, so they went home. But now the spring's here, they're back again.'

At last they reached the wise woman's house. Peter heard George mutter a prayer beneath his breath before they went in, and Peter did the same and touched his charm stone, for it was whispered in the fens that she was a witch. Inside, a peat fire was burning and bunches of herbs hung from the roof. Peter hovered near the door, shy of the wise woman, while George told her, haltingly, why they'd come. She said little, but took the eggs and the wildfowl and laid them carefully down by the fire. Then she measured out some powder from a bowl.

'Has your mother got some brandy?' she asked Peter.

Peter looked nervously round, then he nodded silently. Most of the fendwellers could get a little brandy now and again, but it didn't do to say where it came from. The secret reaches of the fens were well-known to smugglers.

'Good,' went on the wise woman. 'Add a pinch of this to a little brandy; it works miracles on the ague.'

Then she shooed them out of her house and they started back towards the mere.

When they were a good distance from the wise woman's house, Peter asked:

'What's the powder made of?'

'They say it's dried mole, crushed fine. It's best not to ask.'

They walked back the way they'd come and Peter couldn't resist stopping once or twice to look back at the workers as they clambered up and down the steep sides of the new dyke like so many insects. Once, when he stopped, he heard George chuckle beside him:

'Look,' said George, pointing his bent finger.

Peter looked, but all he could see were a group of men crowded at the top of the bank peering down.

'I reckon I know what that's about,' said George, still grinning.

Peter frowned: 'What?'

'I reckon they've struck oak!'

Peter laughed: 'Bog oak! That'll slow them up!'

They both stood and watched, laughing quietly. The fen held many secrets and had a past that could only be guessed at, but once it had certainly been forest; once, thousands of years ago, before the sea had crept so near. And now relics of that forest sometimes reappeared; vast fossilised oaks, hard as iron, sunk deep beneath the surface.

Peter looked up at the wide fen sky. It was getting late; he must hurry back to his mother and sister with the day's catch. He and George walked on, only pausing one more time to look back at the foreigners.

'Vermuyden's gone now,' said Peter. 'So have the others.'

'The mallards!' said George, and they both smiled.

But to himself George thought: 'Mallards. Unsuspecting mallards, ready for the snare. Don't fly away just yet, don't fly away.'

CHAPTER THREE

A light evening mist was descending on the fens as Peter punted silently back along the shortest route. He and George had parted and he was anxious to get home and tell his family about the diggers and Vermuyden.

He tied the punt up to its pole, rammed fast into the mud at the edge of their island, then he lifted out the day's catch and scrambled up the bank towards the house.

Whenever he saw the house, he was filled with pride. His father had built it two summers ago, to replace their old one which had been destroyed by the aegar. Peter had helped his father build this new house; helped build the walls of dried peat squares and the funnel-shaped chimney of braided osiers. His father had made the willow door frame and Peter had woven the reeds under and over to fill the gaps. But it was the roof of which he was most proud – the roof of well laid reeds securely tied down with osiers and ridged with sedge.

Peter paused, as he always did, to look up at the house standing high above the water before he went inside, his bare feet rustling the dried reeds strewn on the floor.

'Where have you been boy? Your mother and sister are waiting to cook.' Peter's father sounded angry.

For answer, Peter laid out his trophies of fish and birds and Meg immediately went to work. His mother was bent over the peat fire and Peter could see how she trembled.

'Mother. I saw the wise woman. I went to see her with Old George. Look what she gave me for your ague.'

His mother turned round and smiled:

'You're a good boy,' she said as she took the powder from him and examined it. 'I know of this new cure. I believe it is better and quicker.'

'Pray God it will work then,' said Peter's father looking anxiously at his wife. She was heavily pregnant again and this time, perhaps, the child might survive. Heaven knew how many babies they had lost since Meg had been born. But it would never survive if its mother still shook with fever as she did now.

While Peter's sister and mother prepared a meal and his father mended a net, Peter told them of what he had seen in the village and on the banks of the new dyke.

'You saw him!' said Meg. 'You actually saw Vermuyden!'

'Yes. And another man with him – and two boys.'

At the mention of Vermuyden, his father frowned and fell silent, so Peter went on quickly to describe instead the visit to the wise woman.

But his father had stopped listening and his eyes were distant.

When they had eaten, Peter, his mother and Meg lay down on their pallets on the floor and drew goat skins over them for warmth. Peter and Meg were soon asleep and, drugged by the wise woman's cure, their mother, too, at last had some rest from the ague. But their father did not sleep. He continued to sit on the floor, wide awake and thoughtful until dawn streaked the sky.

• • • • •

Peter's father had already left the house by the time the others awoke. No-one asked, these days, where he went or what he did, but they all knew. On their island, behind the house, Peter had discovered a well-hidden shelter. He dared not question his father, but he kept his eye on it and one day, when he looked inside, he saw some barrels neatly stacked in the corner. He stared at them for some time, then crept away, frightened for his father. For the barrels were full of powder; powder to be set alight from long fuses of woven sedge dipped in fat.

Plans were afoot for another onslaught on the new dyke.

Peter went down to the edge of the island and saw that the punt was still there. He guessed his father had gone off with Old George and he was pleased because there were many jobs to be done and for most of them he needed the punt. The spring and summer in the fens were busy times; times to prepare for the long cruel winter. There were moles and otters to be trapped for their fur, peat to be cut and stored, sedge to harvest and, as the water receded, the cow to take to the tracts of lush pasture so she could be fattened up before slaughter, then salted down for winter food.

Spring and summer were times, too, for making new boats. Last year, his father had made a coracle for Meg – small and light, like a basket on the water, with skins stretched over its willow frame. It was only big enough for one, and she had become expert at paddling it and learnt how to use the sudden gusts of wind to her advantage. Peter remembered watching her last year, flushed with pleasure at her new skill, as she sped from one clump of bullrushes to another, collecting the bullrush down to stuff into pillows.

This year, Peter's father had promised he would help Peter build his own punt. But now he had other things on his mind.

Peter sighed and went about his work. He wished his father would trust him. He wanted to help destroy the dyke, too. Why couldn't he take George's place? Anyone could see that George was frail and ill. Peter could carry the barrels, stalk the guards and set the fuses just as well as any man.

· · · · ·

But at that very moment at their secret meeting place, his father and Old George, together with some of their most trusted fen tiger friends, were planning a job for Peter which would be far more dangerous than anything any other fenman had ever undertaken.

'I tell you,' said George. 'It's a chance we may never have again. Who knows when Vermuyden will be back? I've only seen him here once before.'

One of the others nodded:

'When he is in these parts, he goes to all the other diggings, too. The Bedford may be the biggest, but there are other cuts all over the fens.'

'That's right' said another. 'And he spends as little time at the diggings as possible. He doesn't like the cold and the damp any more than his workers do!'

'He's always on the move. There's a rumour that it's costing a good deal more than he thought, so he has to keep going to the Earl and his friends for more money.'

'Maybe he'll have to stop the work.'

Peter's father shook his head:

'Not him. Not while there's breath left in him. He's

determined to finish the job, whatever the cost.'

George looked round at the grim unsmiling faces. 'Not while there's breath left in him,' he said.

· · · · ·

It was late in the evening when Peter's father returned and, although it was almost dark, George did not go on to his own home but pulled up his punt onto the island and waited while Peter's father went into the house.

Peter's mother did not rise from her pallet, but she smiled at her husband. They both knew that the baby would come very soon now and Peter's father bent over and stroked her hair with his rough hand, his eyes anxious. Then he turned to Peter:

'Come outside boy. I want to speak to you.'

Meg looked up from the pot she was stirring over the fire, but she said nothing.

Peter went outside with his father. He jumped when he saw Old George standing silent in the twilight like some fenland ghost, but George smiled and patted his back:

'We've something to tell you, lad.'

They walked up towards where the goat and cow were standing at the back of the house and stopped when Peter's father was satisfied that their talk could not be overheard.

The two men sat on the ground and Peter crouched between them, his heart racing. At last he was going to be let into one of their secrets.

· · · · ·

Meg stirred the pot with unnecessary vigour. She

knew, by the way that her father had spoken to Peter just now, that something was afoot. Why should she be left out of their secrets?

She glanced at her mother and saw that she slept again. Quickly, she drew the pot off the fire and crept out of the house then, silent as a polecat, she crawled on all fours until she was near enough to hear what was being said.

• • • • •

Peter's father cleared his throat:

'What we've got to say is serious business, Peter. You must swear that you'll tell no-one – not even your mother or your sister – no-one.'

Peter nodded. His mouth felt dry.

'You know of the fen tigers?'

Peter nodded again.

'And you know that George and I are fen tigers.'

'Yes,' whispered Peter.

'Well, today the fen tigers have made a plan. A very dangerous plan, but if it succeeds, it will almost certainly mean the end of the draining.'

'What!' shouted Peter, forgetting the need for silence.

'Quiet, lad,' said George. 'You'll be no good as a tiger if you shout out like that. Now, listen carefully. We want you to be a spy for us.'

'A spy!'

'Stop repeating everything and listen to George,' said Peter's father impatiently.

George went on:

'When we saw the two Dutchmen with the boys

21

yesterday, it gave me an idea. Today, I talked it over with your father, and found he'd been thinking much the same. So, we met with some of the other tigers and we agreed on a plan. But first we need someone to go and spy out the land for us. We need someone to get friendly with the Dutch boy, the one your age.'

Peter was about to protest, when George continued:

'Now, I know what you're going to say. That no self-respecting fenman would befriend one of *them* and that if he did, the fen folk would slit his throat. Is that right?'

Peter nodded and George smiled approvingly:

'But when you meet the Dutch boy, you'll not be a fenboy. You'll no longer be a yellowbelly, Peter, you'll be an uplander!'

Peter's thoughts were in turmoil:

'But how could I be an uplander? I've the wrong clothes, the wrong talk. Any uplander would spot me as a fenboy!'

'Will you listen!' said Peter's father angrily, and George went on: 'You see Peter, we want to know how long Vermuyden plans to stay here, and when and where he's going. For all we know, he may only stay a day or two, so we need to act fast.

I've been to the village myself today. I found out that he's staying at the inn with the Dutch engineer who is working on the dyke here. That's the other man we saw yesterday and the older boy is his son. The little boy is Vermuyden's son, Cornelius. But as for his future plans, Vermuyden has told no-one. He is no fool and he has learnt to trust no-one except his own countrymen.

No. No man will know of Vermuyden's plans until he has left, but a boy talking to another boy, that's different. They won't bother with you, especially if you're dressed as an uplander.'

At this, George produced a bundle from around his waist and spread it out on the ground. Even in the darkness, Peter could see the jerkin, cap, breeches and boots of an upland boy. *Boots!* No fenman ever wore anything on his feet; nor did they ever wash off the mud. It was considered unlucky – and unnecessary. A fendweller had black feet all the year round, either from the mud or from the rich black dust. The only boots he wore were attached to bone skates when the waters froze.

Peter touched the clothes nervously:

'Where did you get these?'

'That's not your business,' said his father sharply. 'Your business is to wash yourself, change into these clothes, and get to the inn by first light tomorrow.'

Peter bit his lip but said nothing.

'We'll see you get there,' said George kindly. 'We are relying on you.'

'But what if I'm seen by someone I know?'

'The word has been spread. The fen tigers know what your business is. You'll come to no harm from your own people.'

• • • • •

Meg had heard enough. She inched herself from her hiding place and crawled back to the house.

• • • • •

Peter's father stood up:

'Come on in now and eat. It's late.'

23

George also got slowly, painfully, to his feet and went to the water's edge. Peter and his father watched as he slid away into the darkness, knowing his way home by instinct.

As Peter lay under his skins that night and listened to the sounds of the others sleeping, George's words echoed through his mind again and again:

'We're relying on you.'

He shivered and clenched and unclenched his hand.

How on earth could he make friends with the Dutch boy? He tossed and turned, making and rejecting plan after plan. Then suddenly he sat up, his eyes wide. Didn't they realise that tomorrow was May morning when every Godfearing fendweller kept inside?

CHAPTER FOUR

At last Peter slept, but it was a fitful sleep full of terrifying dreams. The final dream frightened him awake and he sat up, rigid and sweating. Then, with mounting terror, he realised that the sound he had heard in his dream was still going on. In the distance, but getting closer, was the sound of a chain rattling.

It was before dawn on May morning. It could only be one thing. The great black ghostly dog who always brought disaster, loosed from his chains, galloping wildly over the fens.

Peter couldn't move for fear. It was some moments before he noticed that his mother was stirring, too. She was moaning quietly, then the birth pangs stopped for a while and she sat up.

This time they both heard the rattling chain.

'Sweet heaven! The black dog!' She put out her hand and clutched Peter's.

They sat side by side, holding each other, waiting for the sound to come closer.

'There it is again!' said Peter.

'But fainter, thank God,' said his mother.

Then the sound faded completely and they both relaxed.

She held Peter to her a moment longer, then she released him:

'Take great care today, my son,' she said.

Peter said nothing. Had his father told her? Surely not.

Yet somehow she knew.

'I will mother,' he said.

'May God go with you,' she whispered, then she lay back again, gripped by a fierce pang.

'The babe will be born today then?' asked Peter.

'Yes my son. Pray for me, and I will pray for you.'

Peter knew he must delay no longer. Dawn was only an hour away and his father had said he must be at the inn by first light. Reluctantly, he went out of the house and down to the water's edge to wash himself. A season's mud caked up to his knees was not easy to remove and it took him precious minutes to get clean. Shivering in the semi-darkness, he went back to the house and put on the unfamiliar clothes. His father was awake and stirring a pot of eels over the fire. Silently he handed some to Peter, then he went to kneel beside the writhing figure of his wife. He spoke gently to her for a moment, then he turned to his son:

'George will take you to the village. Sup your food quickly and go and meet him. I must stay with your mother.'

Although he had little appetite, Peter swallowed the eels and went to the door. His father followed him:

'You make a fine uplander, Peter,' he whispered.

Peter tried to smile, but he was sick with fear.

'God go with you, son,' said his mother.

'And with you, mother,' he replied.

'On your way now,' said his father, then, in a low voice: 'Remember, the tigers are depending on you.'

Peter took one last look at his family – Meg still sleeping peacefully and his mother and father crouched together in mutual anxiety – then he went to the edge of the

island to wait for George.

He didn't have long to wait. George's arrival was heralded by a rasping cough which he tried to suppress, but Peter heard it long before he heard the punt. The punt glided towards the island and Peter was about to wade out to it when George shouted:

'Fool! You're an uplander now. Don't get those boots wet!'

Peter stepped back and looked down at his feet. The boots were loose and of rough leather but they felt like leaden weights to him. He waited for George to get close to the shore, then he stepped gingerly into the punt.

George clapped him on the shoulder:

'You're a brave lad, Peter.'

As they made their way slowly and stealthily from island to island, edging round reed beds and skimming over the shallow water which lay over grass, Peter told George about the black dog.

'You both heard it?' asked George, and his concentration wavered for a moment, making the punt judder from an ill-judged push of the pole.

Peter nodded: 'Yes.'

'It's an ill-omen. Disaster is sure to strike somewhere today.'

Peter knew that as well as any other fendweller. But what he didn't tell George was that it might be a double disaster. Just now, when George had warned him not to wade out to the punt, he had stepped backwards and trodden on a toad with his clumsy uplander boots. And every fenman knows that if you harm a toad ill-luck is sure to follow.

Peter swallowed nervously. Where would disaster fall? On him? On his mother? Or perhaps on both. But he kept his thoughts to himself.

As they got close to the bank where Peter would have to get out and walk to the village, George stopped punting and they both listened, well hidden by the tall reeds. Dawn was beginning to streak the sky and the fen birds were awake. The familiar boom of the bittern sounded through the mist and melted away to be replaced by the note of the reed warbler, and nearby a marsh harrier, with a silvery tail and blue-green wing patches, rose in the sky and hovered before plunging down to take its first fish of the day. But George and Peter were listening out for the sound of humans, not birds.

Satisfied, at last, that there was no-one about, George edged alongside the bank and held the punt steady while Peter scrambled out.

'Remember to keep those boots dry!'.

Peter stood on the bank and looked down at Old George, twisted and shrunken by years of fen ailments. George grinned back at him:

'I'll stay round here all day, lad. Come back when you're ready and give me the signal. You won't see me, but I'll be here, I promise. If you get into trouble, just run for it and I'll be waiting.'

Peter nodded. Their agreed signal was a special bird call, instantly recognisable. Peter knew that Old George wouldn't let him down.

The light was getting stronger now. Raising his hand in farewell, George slipped silently away into the reeds and Peter turned and started to walk to the village.

Not many people were about, and Peter was able to creep undetected into the stable yard at the back of the inn. Here there was plenty of activity. Horses were being fed and watered ready for the day ahead and men and boys were going hither and thither with buckets of water and bundles of hay. There was a great midden heap just inside the yard, steaming and stinking, and Peter hid behind it, watching and waiting. He couldn't remember which horses belonged to the two Dutchmen and the older boy, but he remembered that the little boy had been on a stocky bay pony and he felt sure he'd recognise that again.

The horses were tethered in stalls in a long line and Peter looked up and down the line but he could see no sign of a pony. He looked again, more carefully. It must be there somewhere. The last stall seemed to be empty, but suddenly, Peter saw a movement – the flick of a bay tail. It *was* there! But it was so small it was hidden by the side of the stall.

Peter smiled with relief. At least the Dutchmen were still at the inn. He settled down in his hiding place again, and he was so busy thinking out his plan that he didn't see the forkload of dung being tossed onto the pile beside him. He only just managed to dodge out of the way in time.

At last the yard was silent, except for the sound of the horses munching their hay and shifting in their stalls. The men and boys had gone – at least for the moment. Peter edged his way out of his hiding place and, keeping low, ran across the yard to the stalls. He found a dark corner full of buckets, leather straps and moulding hay, and crouched down to wait. If he could keep out of sight until the Dutch arrived, his plan might work. Although he was dressed as an uplander, the moment he opened his mouth anyone would know him for a fenboy; but the Dutch might not spot the different accent. And on that he was depending.

• • • • •

He had to wait for some time. People came and went and horses clattered in and out of the yard, but there was no sign of the two Dutch boys. Once, Peter heard Dutch being spoken and saw two horses being led out for Vermuyden and the other Dutch engineer, but the boys weren't with them.

Peter had almost decided that his plan was not going to work – that they weren't going to ride that day – when he saw the older Dutch boy come out of the inn and into the yard. He heard him talk to one of the inn servants and was surprised that there was hardly a trace of a Dutch accent in his speech. Quickly, Peter left his dark corner and got into the stall with the bay pony. Snatching a swatch of hay, he started to rub down the animal, keeping his head low.

The Dutch boy and the servant came into the stables and the boy watched as a horse was saddled up for him. He chatted easily to the man, asking him where he should ride, then he noticed Peter and walked up to him.

Peter's heart was hammering so hard it seemed it would burst out of his ribs, but he kept on rubbing while the Dutch boy approached and then stopped outside the stall.

'I haven't seen you here before. Are you new?'

'Yes,' said Peter, trying to disguise his fen accent, 'I started today.'

'What's your name?'

'Peter.'

'My name's Jan. Do you live in the village, Peter?'

Peter nodded and kept rubbing down the bay pony. Jan patted its nose:

'Cornelius is not riding today,' he said. 'He started to cough yesterday, so his father says he must stay at the inn.'

Peter cleared his throat:

'Will you ride out alone then?'

The Dutch boy shrugged:

'Yes, I suppose so. I wanted to go with my father to the diggings, but he said I must stay here and amuse Cornelius.'

'Then why are you riding?'

Jan grinned:

'Cornelius is asleep so I have escaped!'

In spite of himself, Peter found himself smiling in return.

There was a shout from the other end of the stalls:

'Your horse is ready for you, sir. Shall I lead him out?'

'No. I'll take him out myself in a minute,' said Jan.

The servant disappeared and Peter seized his chance:

'Can I ride out with you? I could take the pony.'

Jan looked pleased:

'Yes, I'd like that. Come on then, I'll help you saddle him up.'

Peter had little experience of horses, but Jan didn't seem to notice how awkward he was as they rode out of the yard, through the village and onto the stretch of upland beyond. As they trotted, cantered and then galloped

together, Peter laughed out loud with excitement. He had to keep reminding himself how he hated Jan and all that he stood for.

They turned for home and walked the horses to cool them down. It was easier to talk then, and Peter remembered his mission:

'How long will you stay here, Jan?'

'Only one more day. We shall go back with Cornelius and his father.'

Peter could feel his heart beating faster:

'So you leave the day after tomorrow? Where will you go?'

Peter felt that his question was stilted and unnatural, but Jan didn't seem to suspect anything:

'Go? Why, we shall go back to Fen Drayton. We have a house there now. We used to live in London, so did the Vermuydens, but my father works on the drainage here now, so we have all moved.'

'So you have lived in England for a long time,' said Peter.

'Yes. We have been back to Holland two or three times – to the island of Tholen to visit my grandparents – but I have lived most of my life here.'

As they approached the village, with its distant view of the mere, Jan pointed:

'See, all this water – all this wasteland – one day it will be full of corn and sheep and cattle. He is a brilliant man, Sir Cornelius.'

Peter couldn't help himself. He burst out:

'But it will not be good for the fendwellers. They will have no fish, no reeds, no eels. Their life will be finished.'

'Oh the fen folk. They are mad. It is good to drain the land. What good is a swamp like this? It breeds disease and nothing will grow on it. In Holland, the draining is welcomed by everyone.'

Peter stiffened, but he held his tongue. How could he explain to this Dutch boy? How could he tell him what the fens meant to those who lived among them?

They clattered back into the stable yard and Peter kept his eyes down. He scrambled off the pony's back and led it, and Jan's horse, into their stalls.

'Will you be here tomorrow?' asked Jan.

Peter nodded. He was supposed to be working at the inn, wasn't he? He'd have to pretend he'd be there.

'I'll have Cornelius with me,' said Jan. 'You could help me amuse him. Or will you be working all day?'

There were people about. Peter wanted to slip away as fast as possible.

'I could meet you in the afternoon,' he said quickly, then, almost without thinking, he added: 'Meet me by the mere.'

Jan frowned: 'The mere? Have you a boat?'

Peter thought quickly, desperate to get away from the inn before anyone questioned him:

'I can borrow one,' he said.

Jan smiled broadly.

'I shall enjoy that. Until tomorrow then.'

CHAPTER FIVE

As soon as Jan had gone back into the inn, Peter managed to slip away, unnoticed. He walked quickly out of the village and then ran as fast as his boots would allow, towards the mere. He slid down the bank and, crouching low, well out of sight from any curious bypasser, he gave the special signal.

He waited, but there was no answering bird-call. Peter frowned. He waited a little longer, then repeated it.

Still nothing. No sounds except the familiar ones of water lapping, fen birds about their business, and the rustle of the wind in the reeds.

What had happened? Old George would never desert him; something must have gone wrong.

Again, louder this time, Peter made the signal.

He strained his ears for a reply, looking everywhere amongst the reeds for the hidden punt. Then he thought he glimpsed something, just a faint gleam in the reeds where there should be no gleam. He looked again and saw nothing, but it was enough for his fenman's sixth-sense.

Angrily, he pulled off the stupid boots and, holding them under one arm, he tested the water – once, twice, and then the third time he found what he was looking for; the firm grassy track beneath. As he waded out towards the reeds, the water was up to his waist, but he knew that the track below his feet would hold firm.

As he reached the reeds, he could see where the punt was hidden.

'George?' he called softly. For if it were not George, it might mean trouble.

There was no answer, but, hardly perceptibly, the punt rocked. Peter waded on and, as he approached, he saw the crumpled figure of Old George lying on the bottom of the punt, motionless, with two silver bream beside him – his morning catch. It was the fish which had glinted silver in the sun and betrayed the punt's hiding place.

'George!' Leaning over the punt, Peter shook him, but he didn't respond. His face was grey and a trickle of blood oozed from his mouth.

Quickly, Peter tossed the boots into the punt and pulled himself in after them. He leant over George.

'George. I'm back. I've done the spying. I've found out.'

A flicker passed over George's face and the purple lips tried to move. Peter bent down low:

'Good lad,' George whispered.

Peter felt numb. George was dying. The fens had finally got the better of one of their most skilled sons.

Peter released the punt from the pole and guided it for home as fast as he could, his heart heavy. He took the shortest route, although it meant crossing open water, but he was too anxious to worry about any dangers. As soon as he reached his own island, he pulled up the punt and shouted:

'Father, come quickly. It's George!'

But it was Meg who came out of the house, her face flushed and smiling:

'Peter! Peter – it's a boy! We have a brother. And he's alive! Strong and alive!'

Peter couldn't take it in at first. He stood there, nodding dumbly. Then his father came outside. He put his arm round Peter, then looked at the punt. Together, they went to George. Peter's father bent down and put his head to the frail chest. Then he sighed and stood up:

'Goodbye, old friend,' he said, and his eyes were wet with tears.

For a moment, the three of them stood looking down at Old George, free at last from pain; then Meg, stifling a sob, turned and ran into the house.

At last, Peter's father spoke:

'One fenman dies and another is born.'

Peter nodded.

'Another to carry on the fight,' said his father.

• • • • •

They took Old George back to his people and it was early evening before they returned and Peter was able to tell his father what he'd discovered:

'The day after tomorrow you say? Then we shall have to move fast. They will leave for Fen Drayton at first light, no doubt.'

'What are you going to do, father?' asked Peter. The day had been such a strange one, so full of omens and emotions, that he felt he could ask such a question.

His father looked at him:

'You have proved your manhood today, Peter, proved you are a true fen tiger. I think I can trust you with our secrets.'

Peter looked at his feet and blushed, but his heart was full of pride and he listened as his father explained.

'When they leave the village, they'll follow the new dyke down to Earith. It'll be safe enough for them all along there for the whole dyke is guarded. But once they pass Earith, there's a stretch of fen either side of the river. It's lonely there and a perfect place for an ambush. They'll be easy prey for they'll follow the river and we'll be waiting for them in the fen beside it.'

Peter stared:

'You're going to kill Vermuyden!' he whispered.

His father smiled grimly:

'If we can silence Vermuyden, the diggings will stop. He's behind it all. He's the driving force. I'll murder him with my bare hands – and any other confounded foreigner with him! We shall leave tomorrow morning and we'll be waiting for them not far from Earith.'

'Can I come with you?'

'No, son. You go back and keep faith with the Dutch boy. Meet him by the mere as you arranged. If you don't he may go looking for you at the stables and start asking questions. We don't want the Dutch getting suspicious.'

'Must I go, father?'

'Believe me, son. Your job will be just as important as mine. Now, I must be off to warn the others and make preparations. Look after your mother, Peter. Pray God they both survive this time.'

As Peter watched his father push off from the island, he called:

'The punt, father. I shall need the punt.'

'I shall travel with one of the others. I'll see the punt's here for you.'

Neither of them noticed Meg, her small body expertly hidden among the reeds at the edge of the island.

• • • • •

Peter went into the house and knelt down beside his mother. She was weak but smiling broadly. She showed him his new brother and, indeed, he did look a healthy babe.

'See, Peter. The black dog didn't come for me or for the babe, after all.'

'No,' said Peter, and under his breath he muttered: 'But it came for Old George.'

And the toad's revenge had yet to come.

CHAPTER SIX

The sun was high in the sky when Peter, dressed again as an uplander, cautiously approached the edge of the mere. He hid in the reeds until he heard Jan's voice, talking in Dutch to little Cornelius, then he slid into view.

'Peter!' called Jan and ran to the bank waving his arms:

'I'm so glad to see you. I'm bored of being alone with this little firebrand. I shall be glad when I can hand him back to his mother and his nurse!'

Peter smiled and looked at the dark-haired child jumping up and down beside Jan. He was only about six years old and his eyes were alive with excitement. Peter tried not to think about the tigers and the fen beyond Earith.

Jan and Cornelius scrambled into the punt and Peter pushed off over the mere, his eyes darting from right to left. Not everyone would know of his mission and he didn't want to be seen by his own people if he could help it.

'What are you looking for?' asked Jan.

Peter jumped guiltily:

'It is best to be cautious,' he said. 'You never know who is hiding here.'

Jan smiled: 'My father says the fens hide many things. In the diggings they have found huge oak trees, iron hard, and even bodies preserved in the peat!'

Peter had reached the shelter of the reed bed and relaxed:

'Yes,' he said. 'Outsiders always think they can tame the fen, but they don't know its tricks. There have been Romans and Normans and Danes.' Peter smiled: 'There are plenty of foreigners buried down beneath here.'

'And now more outsiders have come,' said Jan.

Peter blushed, angry with his blunder. He went on quickly:

'There's the treasure of an English king buried somewhere, too!'

Jan leant forward, his eyes alight with interest:

'Tell me about it.'

Peter rammed the punt pole down into the mud and sat down:

'It's a story known all over the fens. It happened hundreds of years ago – not here, but near Wisbech. King John and his soldiers were trying to put down a rebellion by the fen barons. The king and his army crossed the mud flats up there at low tide but they got stuck and many of them were drowned by the tide as it came in over the marshes. All the wagons that carried King John's treasure were sunk.'

'And has no-one ever found any of this treasure?' asked Jan.

Peter shook his head: 'No.'

'It is a strange land.'

While they were talking, little Cornelius was getting restless. He leant over the side of the punt and splashed the water with his hand. Then he found the stilts and tried to lift them up. Jan put them back, then he turned to Peter:

'Who does this punt belong to?'

Peter was scanning the reeds for nests and he answered

without thinking:

'My father.'

Jan said nothing but he looked thoughtful. Peter didn't notice:

'Look,' he said. 'In there. A nest.'

The two Dutch boys knelt up in the punt to look closer. It was the nest of a reed warbler, its grass edges woven around the slender reeds. In the nest lay four small white speckled eggs.

It was a bright afternoon with a light breeze rippling the water. Suddenly, Peter wanted to show Jan more, to make him understand the fierce pride the fen people felt in their watery homeland. As the sun began its downward passage, he took them from place to place; they saw the beautiful black and yellow swallowtail butterfly, a heron wading in the shallows, stabbing at fish and frogs, the Shoveller duck, with its spade-like bill, busy in the muddy water. They even saw a pair of swans, sparkling white in the sunlight, but Peter kept well away from them. He knew better than to anger a cob at nesting-time.

Once or twice they stopped at small islands and Peter showed Jan the fen plants – some in bloom and some still in tight bud. Meadow Rue, Milk Parsley, Fen Ragwort, Marsh Thistle, Great Spearwort, and many many more. Peter knew them all and he knew, too, which could heal and which could harm.

Jan caught some of Peter's enthusiasm. He looked around him at the sparkling water, teeming with hidden life, and up at the sky, big and wide to compensate for the flat land:

'It is beautiful,' he said, 'but how do these fen folk live in the winter? It must be bitter with cold.'

Peter nodded:

'The winters are hard. There are fierce winds blown from the sea and there is fog and ice, too.'

'What do they do in winter?'

'The reeds have to be harvested in winter, and they sew skins, make nets, plait sedge for light.'

'For light?' Jan frowned.

'Yes, the plait of dried sedge is dipped in fat and then lit.'

Peter stuttered as he replied, remembering the fuses behind his house, also made of plaited sedge. Quickly, he went on:

'And they make skates, too. Otter skin boots with runners of sheep bone. On their skates, they can chase the fish that swim under the ice and spear them. It is the only time the fenmen wear anything on their feet, when the fens freeze hard.'

Jan looked at the uplander boots, flung casually into the punt, and at Peter's broad splayed feet. But he said nothing.

They were both silent with their own thoughts, and even Cornelius was quiet, trailing his hand in the sunlit water, so that they were almost upon a mallard's nest before the female sensed their presence and flew heavily upwards sending alarm signals far and wide. Cornelius clapped his hands in delight, and Peter quickly scooped up the eggs and put them into the punt. He watched the mallard fly upward and then skim back onto the water not far away. He remembered how he and George had first seen the Dutch boys and called them puffed up mallard.

'I saw you and Cornelius at the diggings the other day,' he said.

Jan smiled: 'I love to see those diggings. My father has explained everything to me. He has shown me all the drawings and how it will work when it is finished. It is like watching the pieces of a puzzle come together.'

Peter scowled, suddenly full of bitterness. While he'd been punting over the mere with the Dutch boys, showing them the fen creatures and plants, he'd let himself forget why they were here. He had to admit that he liked Jan, he liked his easy ways and his interest in the fens. But he must stop liking him. He clenched his fist and blurted out, rudely:

'When I saw you, I thought you looked like mallard, sitting on your horses in your fancy clothes.'

For a moment, Jan looked puzzled, then he burst out laughing:

'I, too, thought you were like a duck when you rode the pony yesterday,' he said. 'An awkward duck, with your head hunched down on your chest as we galloped.'

Peter frowned. So Jan had noticed! He must have realised that Peter knew nothing of horses! But Jan continued:

'So we are all ducks. All three of us. The three mallard!'

He laughed again and put his arm round Peter's shoulders. In spite of himself, Peter joined in the laughter. He couldn't help it. Jan was full of the joy of life, the joy of a wonderful spring day in the company of a friend, and they both laughed with the sheer pleasure of being young and alive.

Even little Cornelius was infected, and the punt rocked as they all three rolled about with merriment. Cornelius picked up one of the stilts from the bottom of the punt and waved it about, shrieking with excitement.

'Hey,' said Peter, wiping the tears of laughter from his eyes. He grabbed the stilt from the little boy before he could hurt himself or the others.

Cornelius pointed at the stilt:

'What is it?'

'A stilt. For walking on,' said Peter. 'But you need two.' And he picked up the other stilt.

'Show me! Show me!' said Cornelius, bouncing up and down.

'Can you walk on stilts?' asked Jan.

Peter nodded. 'You have to find the firm tracks beneath the water,' he said, and started to prod.

Jan and Cornelius watched as Peter located the track, then swiftly mounted the stilts and walked away from them across the water. Cornelius was thrilled. He clapped his hands together again and again and bounced and wriggled with excitement.

But Jan sat silent in the punt, his open face suddenly serious.

Peter walked back to them, proud of his skill and flushed with pleasure at the little boy's clapping. He dismounted and got back into the punt, hauling the stilts after him.

Jan was sitting very still as Peter reached for the punt pole, then suddenly the Dutch boy put a hand out to stop him. Peter looked up in surprise and met serious young eyes that, only a few minutes ago, had been suffused with laughter.

'You are no uplander, Peter. No upland boy could walk on stilts like that. Even I know that. You are a fenboy aren't you?'

Peter did not drop his gaze but he said nothing.

'You're a fenboy,' went on Jan. 'And the fen people hate us. Why did you make friends with me?'

Then, slowly, the truth dawned:

'It was so you could spy on us for your people!' His voice was suddenly frightened:

'I thought you liked me, but you've been pretending, haven't you?'

'No!' shouted Peter. 'No, I haven't been pretending, I *do* like you, Jan.'

But Jan wasn't listening. Everything started to fall into place:

'You asked me when we were going – and where we were going – and whether Vermuyden was going with us. It's something to do with that, isn't it? The fen people want to know Vermuyden's plans, don't they? What are they going to do to him, Peter?'

His eyes were wide and his hands gripped the edge of the punt.

Still Peter said nothing but his thoughts were racing. Jan had guessed and he was sure to warn Vermuyden, and if Vermuyden was warned, then he'd take plenty of guards with him. Guards that would be on the lookout for an ambush, particularly on that lonely stretch beyond Earith. Peter's father and the other fen tigers wouldn't stand a chance.

For a moment, the two boys stared at each other, bound by a budding friendship but split apart by their backgrounds. Then there was a scream and a splash and they turned, as one, to see Cornelius floundering in the quaking bog not far from the punt.

CHAPTER SEVEN

All other thoughts cast aside, Peter snatched at the pole and brought the punt as near to the little boy as he dared:

'Don't move, Cornelius,' he shouted, for the child was squirming and wriggling, terrified by the treacherous bog which was sucking him under, and the more he fought against it, the further he sank. He was screaming with terror.

Peter acted fast. He lay in the punt and, holding the pole, stretched as far as he could.

'Take hold of the pole, Cornelius. Quickly.'

But the child was sobbing with fright and kept throwing himself about.

'Talk to him in Dutch, Jan,' said Peter. 'If he doesn't hold the pole, he'll go under.'

So Jan pleaded with the child and at last, just as the bog was engulfing his shoulders, Cornelius managed to grasp the end of the pole.

'Now, tell him to hold on. Whatever happens, he must hold onto the pole. Tell him, Jan.'

Cornelius nodded through his sobs as Jan explained, then the two older boys started to pull, very very gently but steadily and firmly, until, little by little, the child's body came free and they managed to haul him, shaken and stinking with mud, but alive, into the punt.

Peter looked down at the little boy, his face streaked with mud and tears, his dark curls sticky and matted, and his body covered with mud. A few seconds more and he would have died. As Jan bent over the sobbing child, Peter knew he could easily tip them both overboard to flounder and be sucked down. That's what his father would have done. Momentarily, he raised the punt pole to strike them, but then Jan turned round, anxious only for the child, everything else forgotten:

'We must get him back to the inn, Peter. Quickly.'

Peter nodded, not trusting himself to speak. His thoughts were in a turmoil as he pulled up the pole, ready to push off, and it was then that he saw a coracle, skilfully hidden, around the side of the reed bed.

As he sped across the mere he looked back. The coracle had moved from the protection of the reeds and Peter caught a glimpse of the figure in it. It was Meg! What was she doing? She should be at the house, caring for their mother. And now instead of going home, she was following them – at a distance, and nearly always out of sight – but definitely following them. Had the coracle been there all the time, the other side of the reed bed? Had she been following them all the time? Peter frowned. He was in enough trouble as it was; he didn't want Meg in it too. If he saw her again, he would shout to her to go home. But she didn't reappear.

• • • • •

When they reached the edge of the mere, they took it in turns to carry Cornelius and made their way to the village as fast as they could. They were the subject of many a curious glance, but Peter was past caring what other folks thought. At last they came to the stable yard.

'We'll go in this way,' said Jan. 'There are less people around.'

But Peter wanted to get away. Somehow he had to warn his father and the other tigers. He had helped get Cornelius to the inn and now he must go. He turned to run, but there was a sudden roar behind him:

'JAN!'

Jan's father and Sir Cornelius Vermuyden had just ridden into the yard! Sir Cornelius leapt off his horse and strode towards them. In a moment, he was beside his son and had gathered him up in his arms, then he turned to Jan and his voice was hard:

'What has happened, Jan?'

'We were on the mere, Sir,' said Jan, 'And Cornelius fell into a bog. Peter here saved his life.'

Peter darted then for the gap between horses and men, but he was caught in a fierce grip by Jan's father.

Sir Cornelius Vermuyden noticed Peter for the first time and he was not deceived. Peter looked back at the strong face with the bushy eyebrows, the long straight nose and the pointed beard.

'He is a fenboy, Jan,' said Vermuyden. 'It is not wise to befriend the fen people.' Then he said to Jan's father:

'Don't let him go. When I've settled the child, I want to speak to him – and to Jan, too.'

And with that he strode into the inn with Cornelius.

· · · · ·

Peter was desperate. He and Jan had been closely questioned by Vermuyden and by Jan's father and, although Peter had given nothing away, he knew that he had still betrayed his people.

He had heard Vermuyden giving orders for guards to accompany him all the way to Fen Drayton in the morning. They had been told to be on the lookout for an ambush from the fen people and Vermuyden had even guessed where that ambush would be.

'We'll play them at their own game,' Vermuyden had said, with a harsh laugh. 'I'm heartily sick of these tiresome fen tigers. We should get all the leaders this time, then they can rot in Ely jail and I can get on with my job.'

Then he'd said to Jan:

'Well Jan, it was a lucky chance that you fell into the fenboy's trap.'

But Jan had said nothing and nor would he look at Peter.

And now it was night-time and Peter was confined to a small room with a guard posted outside the locked door. There was a tiny window, but it was too small to climb through. Vermuyden was taking no chances. He knew that, even now, if Peter escaped, he might somehow warn the tigers so that they could slip away into the fen instead of being overwhelmed by Vermuyden's guards.

He couldn't sleep. All night he paced up and down the bare room or sat, huddled with misery, in a corner. He thought of his mother and Meg back at the house, worrying because he had not returned. He tried to make some plan; think of some way in which he could warn his father, but it was hopeless. There was nothing he could do.

At last, the first light of dawn filtered through the tiny window. Peter got up from his corner and, rubbing his cramped limbs, walked over to the window to look out. The stable yard below was quiet in the half-light. Even the horses weren't stirring yet. He stared listlessly at the scene.

Then suddenly he stiffened, every sense alert again, for coming into the yard was a small figure – a figure wearing a fendweller's hood. It moved swiftly towards the horse stalls and, as it did so, glanced up once towards the sleeping inn, the hood slipping back from the face.

Peter gasped. It was Meg!

What was she doing here? Could she help? For a moment, Peter felt a flutter of hope, but it quickly died. She didn't know enough. If only he could speak to her! He gave a shout, but she didn't stop.

'What's the matter?' The sleepy guard opened the door and peered in. Peter jumped away from the window.

'What are you looking at?'

'Nothing,' said Peter.

Jan was sleeping nearby. He heard the movement of the guard and Peter's voice and he came in.

'We must get ready to go soon,' he said. But he gave the message without looking at Peter.

'Must I come too?' asked Peter, although he already knew the answer.

Jan looked awkward:

'Yes. They want you in case . . .' his voice trailed off.

There was a sound from the yard and the guard looked up:

'What's that? He started to move towards the window but Jan got there first. He looked out and then, turning back into the room, he said:

'They're getting our horses ready.'

But Peter knew he was lying. It was still too early. He knew that Jan had seen the hooded figure hurrying out

of the yard with a stolen horse. He stared at Jan and Jan returned his gaze, but his expression gave nothing away.

· · · · ·

It was some time before the alarm was raised. Peter could hear a great commotion in the yard below, then the sound of someone running inside to tell Vermuyden, and lastly, Vermuyden's voice, raised in anger:

'A fenman's taken it, that's what's happened. He's gone to Earith to warn the tigers!'

'He can't have got far,' said the other man. 'It's been light for less than half an hour and the fen people are bad horsemen.'

'Then get after him, man!' said Vermuyden. 'Take the fastest horse and overtake him. I don't want anyone warning the tigers!'

Peter felt sick with fear. Was Meg really going to ride to Earith? Did she know more than he'd realised? If she was, then she would surely be caught. Poor Meg! What would they do to her!

Then he heard Jan speak:

'Can I go too, Sir? I'd like to give chase. I've got a fast horse and I'm a good rider.'

For a moment, Vermuyden hesitated, then he said:

'Oh very well. I can't deny your horse is one of the fastest. Go now, at once, then. We'll follow you as soon as the guards are ready.'

Peter, still a prisoner, clenched and unclenched his fist. What was Jan up to? He looked out of the window again and saw Jan and the other man clatter out of the yard, already at a canter.

Suddenly all was activity, and it wasn't long before Peter

was mounted, positioned between two guards, and the party for Fen Drayton moved off.

• • • • •

Meg shivered with cold as she bumped along beside the dyke. She clung on grimly to the horse she had stolen, urging it ever faster, kicking its flanks with her legs as she had seen the uplanders do. As the fen awoke and the sounds of the birds grew louder, she looked back over her shoulder to see if she was being followed, but so far there was no sign of pursuit. Once or twice she passed a guard, but they took no notice of her, sleepily assuming she was an upland child, for no fendwellers rode that way. She returned their greetings with a smile, but never spoke.

She was making progress but she ached all over! How much further to Earith? Suddenly, a rabbit got up almost under the horse's feet and bolted away. The horse reared in fright and Meg was unseated. For a moment, she hung on, then she tumbled onto the ground.

She struggled up, tears of hurt and fury streaming down her face. The horse had trotted off and was grazing nearby. It took her precious minutes to catch him and to scramble onto his back, but at last she was on her way again.

• • • • •

Jan and the other man raced along beside the dyke in pursuit, Jan always in front. He sat well down in the saddle, a relaxed and easy horseman, giving the horse its head and trusting it to skirt round any holes or bumps.

'We'll catch the fenman,' said his companion. 'He'll not

have got far. They live like frogs and they ride like frogs!'

Or mallard, thought Jan, smiling to himself. Aloud he said:

'He's had a good start. We may not catch up with him.'

The other man got quieter as they continued to race along with still no sign of a mounted fenman in front.

'If we don't catch him soon, he'll be past Earith,' said Jan, silently hoping that this would, indeed, be the case.

But for answer, his companion suddenly shouted:

'There he is! After him!'

Jan looked and there in the distance was the awkward mounted figure, still bumping along. As he watched, the figure turned and saw them, then it kicked the horse urgently and the bumping canter turned into a gallop, with the small form on top almost flat on the horse's back and hanging on with fierce determination.

Jan kicked his horse on, too. Whatever happened, he must stay in front. He raced ahead fast closing the gap between him and the hooded figure of Meg. But when he had almost reached her, he buried his head on his horse's neck:

'Now boy!' he whispered.

He looked behind to make sure that his companion was far enough away, then, with all his strength, he jerked the rein round and at the same time flung himself out of the saddle and onto the ground.

Reined in at full gallop, Jan's horse reared up and slewed round into the path of the other man whose horse slithered to a halt, unseating its rider.

Jan lay very still on the ground and waited for his

companion to come over to him. The anxious man knelt down beside the boy:

'Jan! Jan, are you all right? What happened?'

Jan moaned, but didn't open his eyes.

And in front of them, Meg rode on, shaking with fright and relief and thanking God for the rabbit hole or the tussock that had, apparently, tripped the horse and, for the moment, stopped her pursuers.

'Not much further,' she whispered to her horse. He was tiring now and she herself was aching and trembling all over.

She patted his neck:

'Just get me past Earith, boy. We can rest then.'

• • • • •

The man didn't know what to do. The boy seemed unconscious. Should he leave him and pursue the fenman or should he stay and tend the boy? As he was more frightened of Vermuyden than of the boy's father, he decided to go after the fenman. After a few more attempts to rouse Jan, he made the boy as comfortable as possible, then he leapt on his horse and headed for Earith as fast as he could.

As soon as he had left, Jan sat up. He rubbed his head and arm for, although he had only feigned unconsciousness, he was badly bruised. He inspected the damage.

'I hope it was worth it,' he muttered. Then he hobbled over to his horse and waited for the others from the inn to catch up.

He didn't have long to wait. They had made good time and he could soon see them approaching along the straight edge of the dyke. When they saw him, two figures detached themselves from the party and galloped ahead – Vermuyden and his father.

'What happened?' shouted his father as he neared Jan.

'My horse tripped and threw me,' said Jan, 'but the other man's gone on ahead.'

Vermuyden looked furious:

'I hope this stupid accident won't spoil our plans,' he said.

Jan caught sight of Peter coming up behind, dwarfed by the two large guards either side of him.

'Even the best riders can fall,' he replied. And although he was speaking to Vermuyden, he was looking at Peter.

• • • • •

As they came to the end of the Bedford Dyke and started to follow the river beyond Earith, Vermuyden forbade anyone to speak. There was no sound except the wind in the reeds, the ever-present birdsong and the snorting of the horses. The guards looked to left and right at the watery fen, but there was no sign of life.

Suddenly, the silence was broken by the shout of a horseman galloping towards them. It was the man who had ridden with Jan.

'The fenman's gone!' he yelled as he got closer. 'I've found the horse, but the fenman's disappeared.'

Very slowly, Peter took his feet from his stirrups. The guards were all looking ahead, looking at the man. In fact, everyone was looking ahead except Jan. Jan was watching Peter as, little by little, he slid off the horse's back. He was almost on the ground when one of the guards started to turn his head.

'Look!' shouted Jan suddenly, pointing up ahead. 'Is that the fenman?'

Immediately, they all looked – and saw nothing. But it gave Peter just enough time. Time to creep away down to the reeds and disappear from sight.

They never found him. At last, Vermuyden and his party moved on towards Fen Drayton. When they were mere specks in the distance, Peter came out of his hiding place and watched them until they were lost to sight.

'Goodbye mallard,' he whispered – but only the wind heard him. Then he turned back to the fen again and gave the haunting bird cry which he knew would bring his father and sister to his side.

PLACES TO VISIT

The Folk Museum, Castle Street, Cambridge
Wicken Fen (original fen), Wicken, Nr. Soham
Welney Wildfowl Refuge
Stretham Steam Engine
The Denver Sluice
Site of Civil War gun battery,
between Old and New Bedford Rivers, Earith.